LITTLE KIWI
COUNTS THE CHICKS

PUFFIN BOOKS

Written and illustrated by
Bob Darroch

It was quiet in the forest.
Not a sound anywhere.

'Where is everyone?'
Little Sister asked.

'They're all at home,' Morepork told them,
'getting ready for their new families.
Listen . . .'

And suddenly there was bird talk everywhere as all the mothers welcomed their new chicks!

Whistle Cheep
Cheep Whistle

Quack Quack
Chee Tweet Tweet Tweet
Chee chee chee
Coo Coo Coo Ki Ki Ki
Ka Ka Ka Chatter Chatter
Chatter Ka Ka Ka Ka Ka Ka Ka
Ek Ek Ek
chirrrrrp Hoot Hoot
Cheep Cheep
Honk Honk Honk

'There must be hundreds,' cried Little Sister.
'Let's go and count them!'

First they found baby Kakapo.

'That's **one**,'
said Little Kiwi.

'And Mrs Morepork has **two**!'

'There are **three** baby Silvereyes!'

four Kaka were already making mischief.

'And **six** baby Bellbirds are learning how to sing.'

eight Parakeets tumbled down to meet them.

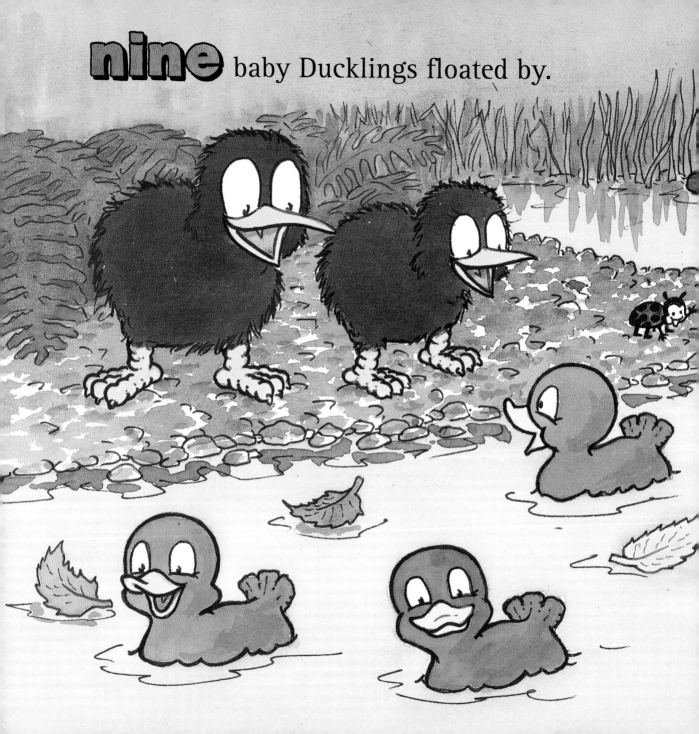

nine baby Ducklings floated by.

And on a branch over the river, **ten** new Kingfishers were getting ready to fly.

Now the forest was filled with the songs of happy chattering chicks.

'How many are there?' an excited Little Sister asked her brother.

'Lots and lots,' he told her.

Little Kiwi couldn't count that many.